067441

x398.2 San Souci, Robert.
S
    The brave little
    tailor

DATE			

The Brave Little Tailor

Adapted from the tale by the Brothers Grimm by **Robert D. San Souci**

Illustrated by **Daniel San Souci**

Doubleday & Company, Inc., Garden City, New York

00B7056

Designed by VIRGINIA M. SOULÉ

Library of Congress Cataloging in Publication Data

San Souci, Robert.
    The brave little tailor.

    Summary: A tailor who kills seven flies with one blow outwits the king and earns half his kingdom and his daughter's hand in marriage.

    [1. Fairy tales. 2. Folklore — Germany] I. San Souci, Daniel, ill. II. Tapfere Schneiderlein. English. III. Title.
PZ8.S248Br [398.2] [E] 81-43427
ISBN 0-385-17569-8 AACR2

Library of Congress Catalog Card Number 81-43427

ISBN: 0-385-17570-1 Trade
ISBN: 0-385-17569-8 Prebound

for Loretta and Yvette
· special thanks to Fred Smaltz·Reidt ·

One summer morning a little tailor sat in his chair by the window sewing a jacket. He was in a good mood and stitched with all his might.

In the street below, an old woman strolled along carrying baskets filled with pots of fresh fruit jam. She sang out, "Good jam—cheap! Good jam—cheap!"

This sounded sweet to the tailor's ears. He stuck his head out the window and cried, "Come up to my shop, good woman, and you'll make yourself a handsome sale."

The woman hauled her heavy baskets up the three long flights of stairs to the tailor's workshop. There he made her unpack every single pot so he could examine them all. He lifted each up, sniffed it, and finally said, "This grape jam looks good to me. Give me four ounces."

The woman gave him what he wanted, but went away grumbling because of the trouble she had gone to over such a small sale.

Meanwhile, the tailor took a loaf of bread from the cupboard, cut himself a slice, and spread it with the jam he had bought.

"This is going to taste *wonderful,*" he told himself, "but before I take a bite, I'm going to finish sewing this jacket."

He put the bread down beside him and went on with his sewing, taking bigger and bigger stitches because he was so eager to sample his jam and bread.

Meanwhile, some flies that had been sitting on the wall smelled the jam and came swarming down onto the bread.

"Hey! Who invited you?" shouted the little tailor, and shooed them away. But the flies refused to stay away and kept coming back in greater and greater numbers.

Finally, at the end of his patience, the tailor grabbed a length of cloth. "Just wait! I'll show you!" he cried, and struck out at them mercilessly. *Flick-flick* went the material.

When the tailor looked down, seven flies lay dead upon the windowsill. Seeing this, he admired his own bravery and exclaimed, "What a man I am!" In his excitement, he decided, "The whole town must hear of my deed."

And one-two-three, he cut out a belt for himself, stitched it up, and embroidered on it in big letters: SEVEN AT ONE BLOW. Then he shook his head and said, "Town, my foot! I want the whole *world* to hear of this!"

So the tailor finished his bread and jam, put on his new belt, and decided to go out into the world, since his shop and his town were too small for such a hero as himself.

Because the world is a large place and a long journey lay before him, he decided to take something to eat along the way. He searched his house for some food, but all he could find was an old chunk of cheese, so he put that into the leather pouch he wore on his new belt. Then he set out.

Just outside his door, he discovered a bird tangled in some bushes. He freed it, and because the tiny creature was exhausted from its struggles, he put it carefully into his pouch beside the cheese.

Then he bravely took to the road; and, since he was light and nimble and in high spirits, he never seemed to get tired.

Up into the mountains he went, and when he reached the highest peak, he found an enormous giant sitting there, enjoying the view.

The little tailor, who wasn't the least bit afraid, went right up to him.

"Greetings, friend," he said. "Looking out at the great world, are you? Well, that's just where I'm headed. Would you like to go with me so we could keep each other company?"

The giant made a face and laughed. "You little pip-squeak! I'd be embarrassed to be seen with such a runt!"

"Is that so?" the little tailor challenged. Then he unbuttoned his coat and showed the giant his belt. "Read that! *That*'ll show you the kind of man I am!"

When he had read SEVEN AT ONE BLOW, the giant thought somewhat better of the little man. He assumed the tailor had laid out seven grown men at one blow. All the same, he decided to test him.

So he picked up a stone and squeezed it until a few drops of water appeared. "Do that," he said, "if you've got the strength."

"That?" the tailor responded. "Why, that's *child's play* for a man like me."

Whereupon he reached into his pouch, took out the soft cheese, and squeezed it until the moisture ran out in a stream.

"What do you think of *that?*" he cried. "Not so bad, eh?"

The giant didn't know what to say. He couldn't believe the little man was so strong. So he picked up a stone and threw it so high that the eye could hardly follow it before it dropped back to earth.

"All right, you little runt, let's see you do *that.*"

"Nice throw," said the tailor, "but it fell to the ground in the end. Watch me throw one that won't ever come back."

So saying, he reached into his pouch again, took out the bird, and tossed it into the air. Fully rested and happy to be set free, the bird flew up and away and didn't come back.

"What do you think of that?" The tailor chuckled.

"I've got to admit you can throw," said the giant. "But now let's see what you can carry."

Pointing to a big tree he had torn out by the roots, he said, "If you're strong enough, help me carry this tree out of the forest."

"Glad to," said the little man. "You take the trunk, and I'll carry the branches—they're the heaviest part."

The giant tossed the trunk over his shoulder; the tailor, however, sat down on a branch so that the giant, who couldn't look around, had to carry the whole tree and the tailor too.

The tailor felt so pleased with his cleverness that he began to whistle a carefree tune, as though hauling trees were nothing to a man of his strength.

After toting his burden for quite a distance, the giant was exhausted.

"Hey!" he yelled, "I've got to drop it!"

The tailor quickly jumped down and put his arms around the tree as if he'd been carrying it and said to the giant, "I wouldn't have thought a tiny tree would be too much for a big man like you."

They continued on together until they came to a cherry tree. The giant grabbed the crown where the cherries were the ripest, pulled it down, handed it to the tailor, and told him to help himself.

But when the giant let go, the treetop snapped back into place and the tailor shot high into the air, falling into some bushes on the other side without hurting himself.

The giant cried out, "What's the matter? You mean you're not strong enough to hold down that bit of a sapling?"

"Not strong enough?" the tailor huffed. "How can you say such a thing about a man who killed seven at one blow? I jumped over the tree to show you how strong my legs are. But *you* try. See if *you* can do it."

The giant tried, but he couldn't clear the cherry tree and got stuck in the upper branches.

Once again the little tailor had come out best.

"All right," said the giant, "if you're so brave, come home with me and spend the night with my family."

When they reached the giant's home, the giant's family was sitting around the fireplace, eating noisily. Grudgingly, they shared their meal with the little man.

After dinner, the giant showed the tailor to a bed and told him to lie down and sleep. But instead of climbing into the oversize bed, he crept into a corner behind an immense chest to keep watch.

At midnight, when the giant thought the tailor must be sound asleep, he got up, took a big oak club, and, in the dark, split the bed in two with one stroke.

"That fixed the little runt," he told his wife as he settled down into his own bed.

In the morning the giants started into the forest to gather wood. All at once the little tailor came striding down the path toward them as bold as could be.

"Run for your lives!" the giant warned his family. "If he survived that blow last night, he must be strong enough to kill us all!"

And they loped away as fast as their legs would carry them.

Laughing to himself, the tailor made his way farther into the world.

After many days, he came to a king's palace. As he stood in the courtyard admiring the buildings around him, the nobles and ladies of the court watched him and read the inscription on his belt: SEVEN AT ONE BLOW.

"Look at *that!*" they said to one another. "What a hero that man is."

Then the king summoned the tailor and said, "Since you're such a great hero, I want to make you an offer. There are two ogres living in a nearby forest. They are laying the kingdom to waste, and they're so ferocious, my knights are afraid to go after them. If such a brave man as yourself would dispose of these ogres, I'll give you my only daughter as your wife, and half my kingdom as her dowry."

"Sounds like just the thing for me," the tailor said. "It's a bargain. I'll get rid of those ogres."

When the king and princess and court marveled at the tailor's courage, he laughed and said, "You can't expect a man who killed seven at one blow to be afraid of two."

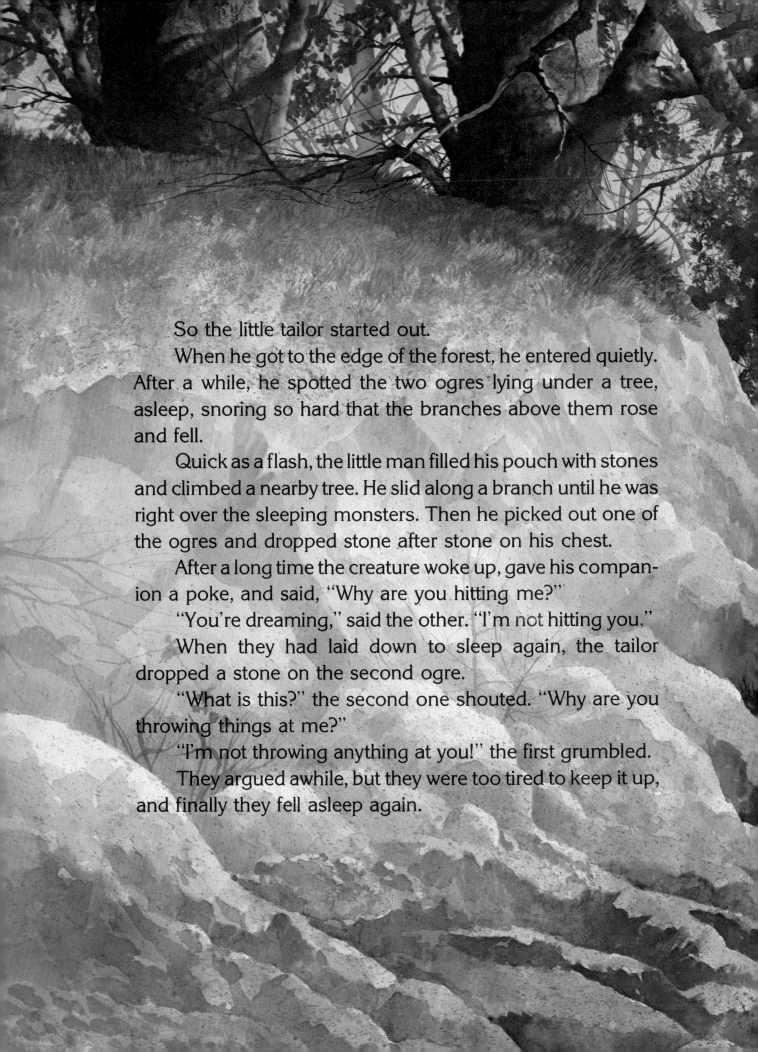

So the little tailor started out.

When he got to the edge of the forest, he entered quietly. After a while, he spotted the two ogres lying under a tree, asleep, snoring so hard that the branches above them rose and fell.

Quick as a flash, the little man filled his pouch with stones and climbed a nearby tree. He slid along a branch until he was right over the sleeping monsters. Then he picked out one of the ogres and dropped stone after stone on his chest.

After a long time the creature woke up, gave his companion a poke, and said, "Why are you hitting me?"

"You're dreaming," said the other. "I'm not hitting you."

When they had laid down to sleep again, the tailor dropped a stone on the second ogre.

"What is this?" the second one shouted. "Why are you throwing things at me?"

"I'm not throwing anything at you!" the first grumbled.

They argued awhile, but they were too tired to keep it up, and finally they fell asleep again.

Then the little tailor took his biggest stone and threw it with all his might at the first ogre's chest.

"This is too much!" bellowed the monster, and jumping up, he pushed his companion so hard against the tree that it shook.

The other shoved him right back, and they both flew into such a rage that they started pulling up trees and pummeling each other. They even uprooted the tree the tailor was hiding in, so that he had to jump to another to save his life.

The ogres kept up the fight until they had pounded each other into so much jelly.

When the forest was quiet again, the tailor jumped down and went back to the king.

"The job is done," he reported. "I've finished them off. But it was a hard fight. They were so desperate, they pulled up trees to battle me with—but how could that help them against a man who killed seven at one blow?"

The king wouldn't believe him at first, so he sent some of his knights into the forest, where they found the ogres lying like grape jam on the ground, with uprooted trees all around.

When the little tailor demanded his reward, the king said, "Before I give away my daughter and half my kingdom, you have to perform one more task. There's a ferocious unicorn loose in the forest. Catch him and bring him to me—*then* you'll get your reward."

The tailor shrugged. "If *two* ogres didn't scare me, why would I worry about *one* unicorn? *Seven* at one blow is my motto."

Taking a rope and an ax, he went into the forest again.

Suddenly the unicorn burst through the underbrush and charged him. But he stood in front of a large tree until the last possible moment, then he jumped quickly out of the way.

The unicorn rammed full force into the trunk, and the creature's horn stuck fast.

Then the tailor put the rope around the unicorn's neck, used his ax to chop the wood away from around the horn, and led the beast to the king.

Deciding it was unwise to provoke such a hero any further, the king gave the tailor the reward he had earned.

The tailor and princess rode to their wedding in a carriage drawn by the unicorn. On the carriage was a coat of arms with a crossed needle-and-thread and scissors on a field of patchwork. At the top was a silver thimble, and below, in gold, the motto: SEVEN AT ONE BLOW!

They were wed with much pomp and joy, and lived as happily as people could in times as uncertain as our own.